GALAPAGOS FUR SEAL
At Home in the Tropics

SMITHSONIAN OCEANIC COLLECTION

To my dear granddaughter, Phoebe Grace, with love—V.S.

To Waldorf schools around the world, especially Haleakala Waldorf School on Maui—A.W.

Book and audio © 2012 Palm Publishing, Norwalk, Connecticut USA, and the Smithsonian Institution, Washington, DC 20560.

Published by Soundprints, an imprint of Palm Publishing, Norwalk, Connecticut USA.
www.soundprints.com

Editor: Jamie McCune
Series design: Shields & Partners, Westport, CT
Book layout: Lindsay Broderick
Audio design: Jamie McCune

Audio Credits:
Performed by Anthony Barone
Produced by Edge Studio

First Edition 2012
10 9 8 7 6 5 4 3 2 1
Printed in China

Acknowledgments:

Carol LeBlanc, *Vice President*, Smithsonian Enterprises
Brigid Ferraro, *Director of Licensing*, Smithsonian Enterprises

Our very special thanks to Don E. Wilson at the Smithsonian Institution for his curatorial review.

Soundprints would like to thank Ellen Nanney and Kealy Wilson at the Smithsonian Institution's
Office of Product Development and Licensing for their help in the creation of this book.

Note: Throughout this book you will find **boldface** words. These words are defined in the back of your book.

Library of Congress Cataloging-in-Publication Data

Sherrow, Victoria.
  Galapagos fur seal : at home in the tropics / by Victoria Sherrow ; illustrated by Anne Wertheim. -- 1st ed.
    p. cm. -- (Smithsonian oceanic collection)
  Summary: Follows two-year-old Fur Seal as he rests on the seashore and swims in shady cave pools during the day, and hunts for food at night. Includes facts about the Galapagos fur seal.
  ISBN 978-1-60727-613-5 (pbk. : alk. paper)
  1. Galapagos fur seal--Juvenile fiction. [1. Galapagos fur seal--Fiction. 2. Seals (Animals)--Fiction. 3. Galapagos Islands--Fiction.] I. Wertheim, Anne, ill. II. Title.
  PZ10.3.S387Gal 2011
  [E]--dc23
                        2011016623

BONUS!
To **download** your audiobook and e-book included **FREE** with your purchase of this book:
1) Go to **www.soundprints.com**
2) Click on "BONUS MATERIALS" at the top of the home page
3) Follow the easy directions!

GALAPAGOS FUR SEAL
At Home in the Tropics

by Victoria Sherrow   Illustrated by Anne Wertheim

Fur Seal awakens from his nap on a rocky ledge. Above him, a **heron** squawks and spreads its long wings. Fur Seal squints in the afternoon sunshine. This tropical island is a hot place for an animal with a thick fur coat. It's time for a swim!

Using all four flippers, Fur Seal makes his way across the rocks. Seawater fills the pools inside the caves on his island home. Fur Seal learned how to keep cool as a **pup** when his mother brought him to these pools. With a splash, he lands in the water and begins to paddle with his flippers.

Fur Seal's sleek body is built for swimming. He leaves trails of silvery bubbles as he dips and spins with the other seals. They swim up, down and around in circles. Sometimes they poke and nip each other as they play.

Darting through the water, Fur Seal looks a bit like a fish, but seals are **mammals**. Mammal mothers give birth to live babies and feed them with their own milk. Mammals also have hair on their bodies. Fur Seal's grown-up coat grew in when he was five months old. It has two layers—long hairs on the outside and short, thick fur next to his skin.

When he is tired, Fur Seal rests in the water. Nearby, crabs scurry sideways along the rocks. They snatch bits of food from the **tide pools**. Oystercatchers and other birds snack on the tiny fish that live in these waters.

The sun hangs low in the sky when Fur Seal leaves the pool. Dinnertime! He walks to the **rookery**, where the seal families gather. Where is his mother? All around him, one-week old seal pups cry out. They are hungry, too. Their mothers have gone hunting in the sea.

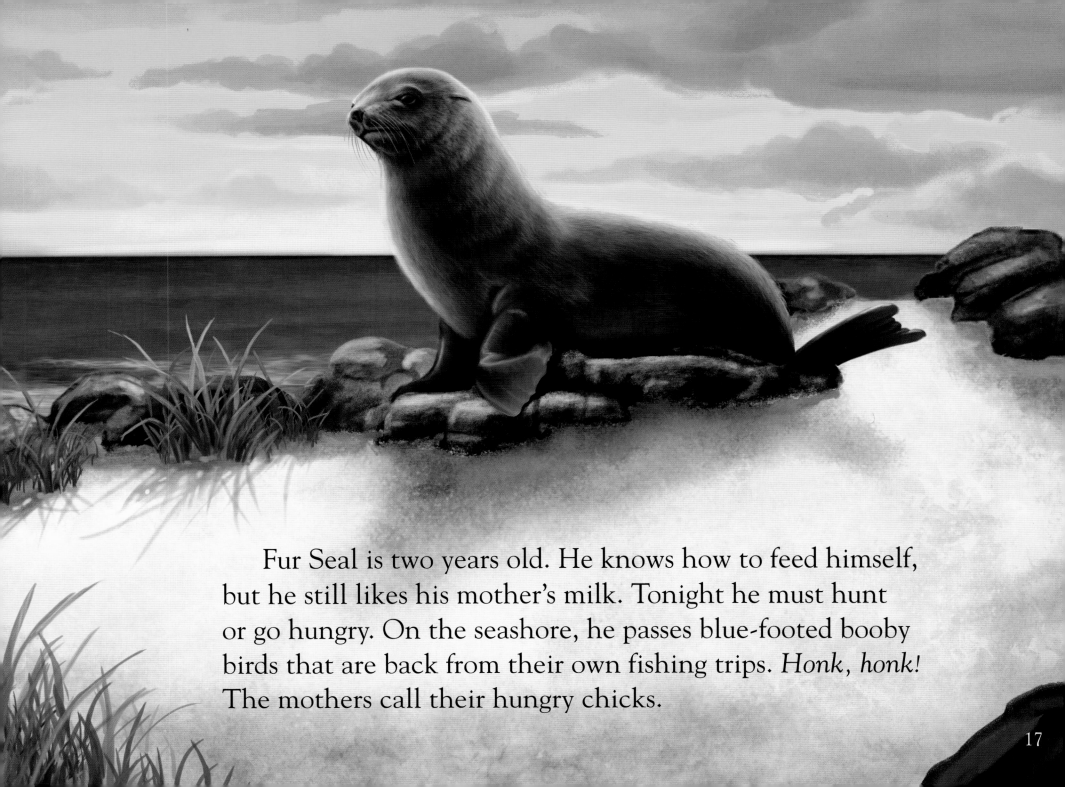

Fur Seal is two years old. He knows how to feed himself, but he still likes his mother's milk. Tonight he must hunt or go hungry. On the seashore, he passes blue-footed booby birds that are back from their own fishing trips. *Honk, honk!* The mothers call their hungry chicks.

As Fur Seal dives back into the water, his small **earflaps** cover his ear holes. His nostrils close, too. Long whiskers will help Fur Seal find fish in the darkness. He hopes he will find enough to eat. Other seals are hunting, too. They are bigger and faster than Fur Seal. Mother seals streak by him and capture small **prey**. An older male beats him to a nearby school of fish.

Fur Seal swims further along the shore searching for food. At last he finds a place where he can hunt alone. He grabs tasty **squid** with his teeth.

After his meal, Fur Seal rests on shore. The booby birds are now sleeping with their wings wrapped around their heads. Night birds coo and hoot. Male sea lions bellow to warn other males to stay away from the mothers and pups that live with them on the beach.

As the sun paints the morning sky, Fur Seal again hunts for food. Foamy white waves crash against the rocks as he swims back to his island. The **marine iguanas** are awake now. They crawl past Fur Seal's resting place and he watches them dive into the water. With arms pressed against their sides, they wriggle their scaly tails. Their heads turn from side to side as they use their small sharp teeth to scrape algae from the ocean floor.

Back on shore, the iguanas snort ocean salt out from their nostrils. Fur Seal moves out of their way and settles down for a nap.

The afternoon brings visitors to Fur Seal's island. A small boat skims across the bay and stops near the beach. People have come to see this special island where only animals live. Friendly birds greet the visitors as they walk around and take pictures.

"Look at the seals and sea lions swimming together!" shouts a boy.

"The seals are smaller than the sea lions," says a girl.

As night falls, Fur Seal again looks for his mother in the crowd of seals. There she is! Fur Seal knows her smell and her voice. But wait—another seal snuggles beside her, drinking her milk. This small seal, with its smooth black coat, is his mother's new pup. When Fur Seal comes near, his mother turns onto her belly and makes noises to send him away. His time for drinking his mother's milk is over. Fur Seal must take care of himself.

Stars glitter overhead as Fur Seal hunts for food once again. He will stay at sea for another day before he returns to his island.

Soon December will come, bringing even hotter days and nights. Cool winds will not blow until May. Fur Seal will escape from the heat in the shady caves and pools. He will swim and play in the water. At night, he will continue to find food in the sea along the rocky shore. He is at home on land or in the water, here in the **Galapagos Islands**.

Fun Facts About the Galapagos Fur Seal

• The Galapagos fur seal is a type of eared seal, meaning that it has small outside earflaps and hind flippers that can turn forward. Using their strong front flippers and these hind flippers, eared seals can move across land and climb the rocky cliffs that are common on their islands. Galapagos fur seals spend about 30 percent of their time in the water while most other seals spend about half of their time in the water.

• People have said that the faces of these seals resemble a bear's. They have short pointed snouts, rounded noses and large dark eyes. Pups have blackish-brown fur, which later ranges from dark brown to dark gray in color when they become adults.

• The Galapagos fur seal is the smallest of all eared seals. Males average 4 feet in length while females are slightly smaller, at 3 feet long. Female seals can begin to breed at about age five and have one pup every one to two years. Scientists think that these seals live up to 20 years.

• These fur seals live in the Galapagos Islands, a chain of small islands located off the west coast of Ecuador in South America. They inhabit the rocky coasts of Isabela, Santa Cruz, Fernandina, and Santiago Island (also called Saint James), where this story takes place.

• At night, the seals dive into the coastal seas to hunt squid and other fish. Galapagos fur seals have been known to dive as deep as 154 feet but they can usually find enough food at depths of 30 to 160 feet below the ocean surface. These dives last about two minutes.

• Galapagos fur seals are rarely attacked by other animals, but they can be hurt by the weather. When temperatures cause the surface of the ocean to become much hotter, their food supply decreases. This happens with a climate event called El Niño.

• Years ago, the seals were also hunted for their skins and oil. The seals are now protected as an endangered species. They number about 20,000.

Glossary

earflap: a small flap of skin forming the external part of the ear in mammals such as seals

Galapagos Islands: a chain of islands off the coast of Ecuador in South America with a population of approximately 23,000 people

heron: a long-legged, coastal bird

mammal: an animal with fur on its body that gives birth to live young, which are fed with mother's milk

marine iguana: a lizard found in, or by the sea, in the Galapagos Islands

prey: an animal that is hunted and captured as food

pup: term used for a baby seal

rookery: a place where animals breed and stay with their young

squid: a type of mollusk with ten arms, or tentacles, attached to its head

tide pool: a pool of water that is left on shore or in a reef after the ocean tide has moved away

Points of Interest in this Book

pp. 4-5: yellow-crowned night heron
pp. 6-7: cave pools
pp. 12-13: Sally Lightfoot crabs; oyster-catchers; swallow-tailed gulls

pp. 16-17, 22-23: blue-footed booby birds
pp. 22-23, 26-27: sea lions
pp. 24-25, 26-27: marine iguanas